ROCKFORD PUBLIC LIBRARY
D1072421

WITHDRAWN

Short Vowel Phonics 3: Ants in the Grass

and other tales

Double Consonants and "-ing"

by: Patricia J. Norton

illustrated by: Sarah E. Cashman

Notes to Parents and Teachers:

Short Vowel Phonics 3 is the next book after Short Vowel Phonics 2. In this book the reader will experience 3 new concepts:

1) double consonants
2) "-ing" in words (king, ring, spring etc.)
3) "-ing" as a suffix

One new non-phonic sight word is added: of

Previous non-phonic sight words: a, as, has, his, is, the

Other reading material by the Author:

Short Vowel Phonics 1
Short Vowel Phonics 2
Short Vowel Phonics 4
Short Vowel Phonics Short Stories
Decodable Alphabet Chart

ISBN: 978-0-9817710-3-8 (lib. bdg.)
3rd printing
[1. Reading - Phonetic method. 2. Reading readiness. 3. Phonics]

Illustrated by Sarah E. Cashman

Printed in Springfield, Missouri, U. S. A.

Text font: Pen Time Manuscript

Table of Contents

Double Consonants

Chapter 7:

Summing It Up — Page 25

Poems inspired by Short Vowel Phonics 2's stories
New concept: "-ing" as a suffix
Sight words: a ,has, his, is, of, the
Vocabulary Preview: pant (verb), slack,
daft, drift (noun)

Jin (j ĭn) a male Chinese name that means <u>gold</u>.

Pam and Fran Pant — Page 25
word count: 30

Brad the Lad — Page 26
word count: 29

Jin Digs — Page 26
word count: 33

Bud the Pup — Page 27
word count: 34

The Sled — Page 28
word count: 29

Chapter 1

Ants in the Grass

Ants sat in a box of sand. The box had an ant clan. The clan had Ann, Matt, Grant, and Jack.

The clan of ants ran in the grass. The ants ran past a cat. And the ants ran past a brass box. The clan ran in the grass. In the grass sat a sack.

The sack had buns and jam. The sack had a mass of black ants. The sack had an ant trap.

Ann, the ant: "A trap! A trap! Back! Get back!"

The clan of ants ran fast.

The ants ran past the brass

box. The ants ran past the cat. The ant clan ran at the box of sand.

"Pant! Pant! Pant!" Ann, Matt, Grant, and Jack pant in the box of sand.

The sand lacks an ant trap. Grant, the ant: "Sand is grand!"

Chapter 2

Rent a Tent

Jeff had a tent. Jeff and Brett went and set up the tent.

Jeff and Brett crept in and slept. As Jeff and Brett slept, a pest went in the tent. "Yelp!" went Jeff and Brett. The pest fled the tent. Brett fled the tent.

Jeff: "A bed is best." Jeff went and slept in his bed. Brett went and slept in his bed. And Jeff's pet went and slept in the tent.

Jeff gets up. Brett gets up. Jeff and Brett step in the tent. Brett: "Jeff, the tent is a mess. The tent has a rent."

Jeff mends the rent. Jeff sets up the tent. Jeff tests the tent. The tent bends. Brett yells, "The tent fell!" Jeff frets.

Brett helps Jeff. Brett steps on the tent pegs. Brett

tests the tent. Brett yells, "Yes, the tent held!" The tent is swell.

In the end, Brett helps Jeff rent the tent.

Chapter 3

Can Vic Fix It?

Vic has a big rig. And Jill Quinn has a pig.

Vic is in his rig.

HISS. FIZZ. Bam, bam, BAM. Crack. Drip, drip.

The rig is still. The rig quits. Vic is in a bad fix. Can Vic fix his big rig? Vic can fix it.

Vic is in his rig. The rig is at the hill. Jill's pig is at the hill. Will Vic miss the pig? The rig zig-zags. The rig hits the pig. The pig quits. The pig is ham!

Miss Quinn has a fit. Can Vic fix it?

Vic has yams in his rig. Jill sits and has a yam. Vic sits and has the ham.

Chapter 4

Mom, Tom and Jon Frost

Mom: "Tom! Jon! Mom has jobs."

Jon got Bonn, the dog, and had a jog.

Mom: "Tom, slop the hogs."

Tom: "Stop the hogs?"

Mom: "Not! Tom, slop the hogs."

Tom: "Slop the frogs?"

Mom: "Tom Scott, slop the hogs."

Tom slops the hogs.

Mom: "Jon, JON ROSS."

Clomp, clomp, clomp.

Jon: "Mom?"

Mom: "Jon, mop the hog lot."

Jon: "<u>Flop</u> the hog lot?"

Mom: "Not! Jon, mop the hog lot."

Jon: "Mop the <u>smog</u> lot?"

Mom: "Jon Ross Frost, mop the hog lot."

Mom is the boss. Jon mops the hog lot. And Mom drops on a cot.

Chapter 5

Stuff

Miss Bess Dunn has a lot of stuff.

Mom Dunn has a fuss. Mom is gruff and tells Bess: "Get rid of the stuff." It is not a bluff. Mom is in a huff.

Bess runs and gets a red dress. Mom runs and gets a red truck.

Mom sets the stuff in the back of the truck.

Mom gets in the truck. At the "Stop and Sell–It Spot," Mom sells a lot of stuff. Mom dumps the rest of the stuff at the dump.

Miss Dunn will miss the stuff. But less stuff is Mom's bliss.

Chapter 6

The King in Spring

It is spring. The king plans a trip. The king brings his sling on the trip.

The king has a rock in the sling. The king swings his sling. The rock hits a bell. The bell rings.

The king has a rock in his sling. The rock hits a

pond. The rock skips on the pond.

The king has a rock in his sling. The rock hits a tin ring. The ring: "Ping, ping."

"A grand sling!" sings the king.

Summing It Up

Pam and Fran Pant

The pals did run on a track.

In running Fran did not slack.

But Pam is fast, and Pam ran.

A panting Pam ran past Fran.

Brad the Lad

A lad can nap on a raft.

Napping, rafting? Is Brad daft?

Not daft, not him! It is fun.

The lad can nap in the sun.

....

Jin Digs

The kid will dig a big, big pit.

A ding! Jin's digging has a hit.

The lad has hit a black tin box.

Has it a ring? a pin? his socks?

Bud the Pup

A frog did jump in lots of mud.

His jumping got the mud

on Bud.

Up in the tub the dog is sent.

On Bud a lot of suds is spent.

The Sled

Meg's sled is big and red.

On hills the sled has sped.

The lass is sledding fast and swift.

Till Meg did hit a big, big drift.